Breeds of Dogs

Written by
Stephen Rickard

Labrador

This breed of dog is a Labrador.

A Labrador, or "lab" for short, can be a good pet.

Labradors are good hunting dogs.

They are big dogs and can run and swim well.

Labrador pups

Chow Chow

This dog is a Chow Chow.

It is a strong dog with thick fur.

The Chow Chow has ears that stick up. They are a bit like the ears of a panda.

A Chow Chow pup

Sheepdog

Sheepdogs are the best dogs
for gathering sheep.
Farmers have sheepdogs on the farm.

Some sheepdogs need to run a lot.

Sheepdogs are smart.
They can understand
the farmer. They can do
what the farmer tells
them to do.

Pug

This breed of dog is a Pug.

Pugs are not big dogs.
Pugs have a tail with a curl in it.

Pugs need to run a lot.
Pugs that do not run a lot will get fat.

Boxer

This breed of dog is a Boxer.

Boxer dogs are big and strong, with short tails.

They can be good pets.

Akita ("A-keeta")

This dog is an Akita.

This dog is from Japan.
It is a hunting dog.

This big, strong dog has a thick fur coat.

Shih Tzu ("Shi ts-zoo")

This dog is a Shih Tzu.

It is a little dog with a soft coat.
The coat can get long, so it must be cut.

You need to brush Shih Tzus a lot too.

Shih Tzus do not need to run much.
They are good pets.

What dog will you have?